December 2003

J. M. COETZEE

Lecture and

Speech of Acceptance

Upon the Award

of the

Nobel Prize in Literature,

Delivered in Stockholm

in December

2003

PENGUIN BOOKS

2004

PENGUIN BOOKS

Published by the Penguin Group

Penguin Group (USA) Inc., 375 Hudson Street,
New York, New York 10014, U.S.A

Penguin Group (Canada), 10 Alcorn Avenue, Toronto, Ontario,
Canada M4V 3B2 (a division of Pearson Penguin Canada Inc.)

Penguin Books Ltd, 80 Strand, London WC2R 0RL, England

Penguin Ireland, 25 St Stephen's Green, Dublin 2, Ireland
(a division of Penguin Books Ltd)

Penguin Group (Australia), 250 Camberwell Road, Camberwell,
Victoria 3124, Australia (a division of Pearson Australia Group Pty Ltd)

Penguin Books India Pvt Ltd, 11 Community Centre, Panchsheel Park,
New Delhi–110 017, India

Penguin Group (NZ), cnr Airborne and Rosedale Roads, Albany,
Auckland, New Zealand (a division of Pearson New Zealand Ltd)

Penguin Books (South Africa) (Pty) Ltd, 24 Sturdee Avenue,
Rosebank, Johannesburg 2196, South Africa

Penguin Books Ltd, Registered Offices:
80 Strand, London WC2R 0RL, England

First published in Penguin Books 2004

1 3 5 7 9 10 8 6 4 2

CIP data available
ISBN 0 14 30.3453 7

Printed in Mexico
Set in Dante
Designed by Francesca Belanger

J. M. Coetzee, "who in innumerable guises portrays the surprising involvement of the outsider."

—The Swedish Academy

J. M. Coetzee—Nobel Lecture

HE AND HIS MAN

But to return to my new companion. I was greatly de-lighted with him, and made it my business to teach him everything that was proper to make him useful, handy, and helpful; but especially to make him speak, and understand me when I spoke; and he was the aptest scholar there ever was.

—Daniel Defoe, *Robinson Crusoe*

BOSTON, on the coast of Lincolnshire, is a handsome town, writes his man. The tallest church steeple in all of England is to be found there; sea-pilots use it to navigate by. Around Boston is fen country. Bitterns abound, ominous birds who give a heavy, groaning call loud enough to be heard two miles away, like the report of a gun.

The fens are home to many other kinds of birds too, writes his man, duck and mallard, teal and widgeon, to capture which the men of the fens, the fen-men, raise tame ducks, which they call decoy ducks or duckoys.

■   ■   ■

Fens are tracts of wetland. There are tracts of wetland all over Europe, all over the world, but they are not named fens, fen is an English word, it will not migrate.

These Lincolnshire duckoys, writes his man, are bred up in decoy ponds, and kept tame by being fed by hand. Then when the season comes they are sent abroad to Holland and Germany. In Holland and Germany they meet with others of their kind, and, seeing how miserably these Dutch and German ducks live, how their rivers freeze in winter and their lands are covered in snow, fail not to let them know, in a form of language which they make them understand, that in England from where they come the case is quite otherwise: English ducks have seashores full of nourishing food, tides that flow freely up the creeks; they have lakes, springs, open ponds and sheltered ponds; also lands full of corn left behind by the gleaners; and no frost or snow, or very light.

By these representations, he writes, which are made all in duck language, they, the decoy ducks or duckoys, draw together vast numbers of fowl and, so to say, kidnap them. They guide them back across the seas from Holland and Germany and settle them down in their decoy ponds on the fens of Lincolnshire, chattering and gabbling to them all the time in their own language, telling them these are the ponds they told them of, where they shall live safely and securely.

And while they are so occupied the decoy-men, the masters of the decoy ducks, creep into covers or coverts they have built of reeds upon the fens, and all unseen toss handfuls of corn upon the water; and the decoy ducks or duckoys follow them, bringing their foreign guests behind. And so over two or three days they lead their guests up narrower and narrower waterways, calling to them all the time to see how well we live in England, to a place where nets have been spanned.

Then the decoy-men send out their decoy dog, which has been perfectly trained to swim after fowl, barking as he swims. Being alarmed to the last degree by this terrible creature, the ducks take to the wing, but are forced down again into the water by the arched nets above, and so must swim or perish, under the net. But the net grows narrower and narrower, like a purse, and at the end stand the decoy-men, who take their captives out one by one. The decoy ducks are stroked and made much of, but as for their guests, these are clubbed on the spot and plucked and sold by the hundred and by the thousand.

All of this news of Lincolnshire his man writes in a neat, quick hand, with quills that he sharpens with his little penknife each day before a new bout with the page.

In Halifax, writes his man, there stood, until it was removed in the reign of King James the First, an engine of execution, which worked thus. The condemned man was laid with his head on the cross-base or cup of the scaffold; then the executioner knocked out a pin which held up the heavy blade. The blade descended down a frame as tall as a church door and beheaded the man as clean as a butcher's knife.

Custom had it in Halifax, though, that if between the knocking out of the pin and the descent of the blade the condemned man could leap to his feet, run down the hill, and swim across the river without being seized again by the executioner, he would be let free. But in all the years the engine stood in Halifax this never happened.

He (not *his man* now but *he*) sits in his room by the waterside in Bristol and reads this. He is getting on in years, almost it might be said he is an old man by now. The skin of his face, that had been almost blackened by the tropic sun before he made a parasol out of palm or palmetto leaves to shade himself, is paler now, but still leathery like parchment; on his nose is a sore from the sun that will not heal.

The parasol he has still with him in his room, standing in a corner, but the parrot that came back with him has passed away. *Poor Robin!* the parrot would squawk from its perch on his shoulder, *Poor Robin Crusoe! Who shall save poor Robin?* His wife could not abide the lamenting of the parrot, *Poor Robin* day in, day out. *I shall wring its neck,* said she, but she had not the courage to do so.

When he came back to England from his island with his parrot and his parasol and his chest full of treasure, he lived for a while tranquilly enough with his old wife on the estate he bought in Huntingdon, for he had become a wealthy man, and wealthier still after the printing of the book of his adventures. But the years on the island, and then the years traveling with his serving-man Friday (poor Friday, he laments to himself, squawk-squawk, for the parrot would never speak Friday's name, only his), had made the life of a landed gentleman dull for him. And, if the truth be told, married life was a sore disappointment too. He found himself retreating more and more to the stables, to his horses, which blessedly did not chatter, but whinnied softly when he came, to show that they knew who he was, and then held their peace.

It seemed to him, coming from his island, where until Friday arrived he lived a silent life, that there was too much speech in the world. In bed beside his wife he felt as if a shower of pebbles were being poured upon his head, in an unending rustle and clatter, when all he desired was to sleep.

So when his old wife gave up the ghost he mourned but was not sorry. He buried her and after a decent while took this room in *The Jolly Tar* on the Bristol waterfront, leaving the direction of the estate in Huntingdon to his son, bringing with him only the parasol from the island that made him famous and the dead parrot fixed to its perch and a few necessaries, and has lived here alone ever since, strolling by day about the wharves and quays, staring out west over the sea, for his sight is still keen, smoking his pipes. As to his meals, he has these brought up to his room; for he finds no joy in society, having grown used to solitude on the island.

He does not read, he has lost the taste for it; but the writing of his adventures has put him in the habit of writing, it is a pleasant enough recreation. In the evening by candlelight he will take out his papers and sharpen his quills and write a page or two of his man, the man who sends report of the duckoys of Lincolnshire, and of the great engine of death in Halifax, that one can escape if before the awful blade can descend one can leap to one's feet and dash down the hill, and of numbers of other things. Every place he goes he sends report of—that is his first business, this busy man of his.

Strolling along the harbour wall, reflecting upon the engine from Halifax, he, Robin, whom the parrot used to call poor Robin, drops a pebble and listens. A second, less than a second, before it strikes the water. God's grace is swift, but might not the great blade of tempered steel, being heavier than a pebble and being greased with tallow, be swifter? How will we ever escape it? And what species of man can it be who will dash so busily hither and thither across the kingdom, from one spectacle of death to another (clubbings, beheadings), sending in report after report?

A man of business, he thinks to himself. Let him be a man of business, a grain merchant or a leather merchant, let us say; or a manufacturer and purveyor of roof tiles somewhere where clay is plentiful, Wapping let us say, who must travel much in the interest of his trade. Make him prosperous, give him a wife who loves him and does not chatter too much and bears him children, daughters mainly; give him a reasonable happiness; then bring his happiness suddenly to an end. The Thames rises one winter, the kilns in which the tiles are baked are washed away, or the grain stores, or the leather works; he is ruined, this man of his, debtors descend upon him like flies or like crows, he has to flee his home, his wife, his children, and seek hiding in the most wretched of quarters in Beggars Lane under a false name and in disguise. And all of this—the wave of water, the ruin, the flight, the pennilessness, the tatters, the solitude—let all of this be a figure of the shipwreck and the island where he, poor Robin, was secluded from the world for twenty-six years, till he almost went mad (and indeed, who is to say he did not, in some measure?).

Or else let the man be a saddler with a home and a shop and a warehouse in Whitechapel and a mole on his chin and a wife who loves him and does not chatter and bears him children, daughters mainly, and gives him much happiness, until the plague descends upon the city, it is the year 1665, the great fire of London has not yet come. The plague descends upon London: daily, parish by parish, the count of the dead mounts, rich and poor, for the plague makes no distinction among stations, all this saddler's worldly wealth will not save him. He sends his wife and daughters into the countryside and makes plans to flee himself, but then does not. *Thou shalt not be afraid for the terror at night,* he reads, opening the Bible at hazard, *not for the arrow that flieth by day; not for the pestilence that walketh in darkness; nor for the destruction that wasteth at noon-day. A thousand shall fall at thy side, and ten thousand at thy right hand, but it shall not come nigh thee.*

Taking heart from this sign, a sign of safe passage, he remains in afflicted London and sets about writing reports. I came upon a crowd in the street, he writes, and a woman in their midst pointing to the heavens. *See,* she cries, *an angel in white brandishing a flaming sword!* And the crowd all nod among themselves, *Indeed it is so,* they say: *an angel with a sword!* But he, the saddler, can see no angel, no sword. All he can see is a strange-shaped cloud brighter on the one side than the other, from the shining of the sun.

It is an allegory! cries the woman in the street; but he can see no allegory for the life of him. Thus in his report.

On another day, walking by the riverside in Wapping, his man that used to be a saddler but now has no occupation observes how a woman from the door of her house calls out to a man rowing in a dory: *Robert! Robert!* she calls; and how the man then rows ashore, and from the dory takes up a sack which he lays upon a stone by the riverside, and rows away again; and how the woman comes down to the riverside and picks up the sack and bears it home, very sorrowful-looking.

He accosts the man Robert and speaks to him. Robert informs him that the woman is his wife and the sack holds a week's supplies for her and their children, meat and meal and butter; but that he dare not approach nearer, for all of them, wife and children, have the plague upon them; and that it breaks his heart. And all of this— the man Robert and wife keeping communion through calls across the water, the sack left by the waterside—stands for itself certainly, but stands also as a figure of his, Robinson's, solitude on his island, where in his hour of darkest despair he called out across the waves to his loved ones in England to save him, and at other times swam out to the wreck in search of supplies.

Further report from that time of woe. Able no longer to bear the pain from the swellings in the groin and armpit that are the signs of the plague, a man runs out howling, stark naked, into the street, into Harrow Alley in Whitechapel, where his man the saddler witnesses him as he leaps and prances and makes a thousand strange gestures, his wife and children running after him crying out, calling to him to come back. And this leaping and prancing is allegoric of his own leaping and prancing when, after the calamity of the shipwreck and after he had scoured the strand for sign of his shipboard companions and found none, save a pair of shoes that were not mates, he had understood he was cast up all alone on a savage island, likely to perish and with no hope of salvation.

(But of what else does he secretly sing, he wonders to himself, this poor afflicted man of whom he reads, besides his desolation? What is he calling, across the waters and across the years, out of his private fire?)

A year ago he, Robinson, paid two guineas to a sailor for a parrot the sailor had brought back from, he said, Brazil—a bird not so magnificent as his own well-beloved creature but splendid nonetheless, with green feathers and a scarlet crest and a great talker too, if the sailor was to be believed. And indeed the bird would sit on its perch in his room in the inn, with a little chain on its leg in case it should try to fly away, and say the words *Poor Poll! Poor Poll!* over and over till he was forced to hood it; but could not be taught to say any other word—*Poor Robin!* for instance—being perhaps too old for that.

Poor Poll, gazing out through the narrow window over the mast-tops and, beyond the mast-tops, over the grey Atlantic swell: *What island is this,* asks Poor Poll, *that I am cast up on, so cold, so dreary? Where were you, my Saviour, in my hour of great need?*

A man, being drunk and it being late at night (another of his man's reports), falls asleep in a doorway in Cripplegate. The dead-cart comes on its way (we are still in the year of the plague), and the neighbours, thinking the man dead, place him on the dead-cart among the corpses. By and by the cart comes to the dead pit at Mountmill and the carter, his face all muffled against the effluvium, lays hold of him to throw him in; and he wakes up and struggles in his bewilderment. *Where am I?* he says. *You are about to be buried among the dead,* says the carter. *But am I dead then?* says the man. And this too is a figure of him on his island.

Some London-folk continue to go about their business, thinking they are healthy and will be passed over. But secretly they have the plague in their blood: when the infection reaches their heart they fall dead upon the spot, so reports his man, as if struck by lightning. And this is a figure for life itself, the whole of life. Due preparation. We should make due preparation for death, or else be struck down where we stand. As he, Robinson, was made to see when of a sudden, on his island, he came one day upon the footprint of a man in the sand. It was a print, and therefore a sign: of a foot, of a man. But it was a sign of much else too. *You are not alone,* said the sign; and also, *No matter how far you sail, no matter where you hide, you will be searched out.*

In the year of the plague, writes his man, others, out of terror, abandoned all, their homes, their wives and children, and fled as far from London as they could. When the plague had passed, their flight was condemned as cowardice on all sides. But, writes his man, we forget what kind of courage was called on to confront the plague. It was not a mere soldier's courage, like gripping a weapon and charging the foe: it was like charging Death himself on his pale horse.

Even at his best, his island parrot, the better loved of the two, spoke no word he was not taught to speak by his master. How then has it come about that this man of his, who is a kind of parrot and not much loved, writes as well as or better than his master? For he wields an able pen, this man of his, no doubt of that. *Like charging Death himself on his pale horse.* His own skill, learned in the counting house, was in making tallies and accounts, not in turning phrases. *Death himself on his pale horse:* those are words he would not think of. Only when he yields himself up to this man of his do such words come.

And decoy ducks, or duckoys: What did he, Robinson, know of decoy ducks? Nothing at all, until this man of his began sending in reports.

The duckoys of the Lincolnshire fens, the great engine of execution in Halifax: reports from a great tour this man of his seems to be making of the island of Britain, which is a figure of the tour he made of his own island in the skiff he built, the tour that showed there was a farther side to the island, craggy and dark and inhospitable, which he ever afterwards avoided, though if in the future colonists shall arrive upon the island they will perhaps explore it and settle it; that too being a figure, of the dark side of the soul and the light.

When the first bands of plagiarists and imitators descended upon his island history and foisted on the public their own feigned stories of the castaway life, they seemed to him no more or less than a horde of cannibals falling upon his own flesh, that is to say, his life; and he did not scruple to say so. *When I defended myself against the cannibals, who sought to strike me down and roast me and devour me,* he wrote, *I thought I defended myself against the thing itself. Little did I guess,* he wrote, *that these cannibals were but figures of a more devilish voracity, that would gnaw at the very substance of truth.*

But now, reflecting further, there begins to creep into his breast a touch of fellow-feeling for his imitators. For it seems to him now that there are but a handful of stories in the world; and if the young are to be forbidden to prey upon the old then they must sit forever in silence.

■   ■   ■

Thus in the narrative of his island adventures he tells of how he awoke in terror one night convinced the devil lay upon him in his bed in the shape of a huge dog. So he leapt to his feet and grasped a cutlass and slashed left and right to defend himself while the poor parrot that slept by his bedside shrieked in alarm. Only many days later did he understand that neither dog nor devil had lain upon him, but rather that he had suffered a palsy of a passing kind, and being unable to move his leg had concluded there was some creature stretched out upon it. Of which event the lesson would seem to be that all afflictions, including the palsy, come from the devil and are the very devil; that a visitation by illness may be figured as a visitation by the devil, or by a dog figuring the devil, and vice versa, the visitation figured as an illness, as in the saddler's history of the plague; and therefore that no one who writes stories of either, the devil or the plague, should forthwith be dismissed as a forger or a thief.

■   ■   ■

When, years ago, he resolved to set down on paper the story of his island, he found that the words would not come, the pen would not flow, his very fingers were stiff and reluctant. But day by day, step by step, he mastered the writing business, until by the time of his adventures with Friday in the frozen north the pages were rolling off easily, even thoughtlessly.

That old ease of composition has, alas, deserted him. When he seats himself at the little writing-desk before the window looking over Bristol harbour, his hand feels as clumsy and the pen as foreign an instrument as ever before.

Does he, the other one, that man of his, find the writing business easier? The stories he writes of ducks and machines of death and London under the plague flow prettily enough; but then so did his own stories once. Perhaps he misjudges him, that dapper little man with the quick step and the mole upon his chin. Perhaps at this very moment he sits alone in a hired room somewhere in this wide kingdom dipping the pen and dipping it again, full of doubts and hesitations and second thoughts.

How are they to be figured, this man and he? As master and slave? As brothers, twin brothers? As comrades in arms? Or as enemies, foes? What name shall he give this nameless fellow with whom he shares his evenings and sometimes his nights too, who is absent only in the daytime, when he, Robin, walks the quays inspecting the new arrivals and his man gallops about the kingdom making his inspections?

Will this man, in the course of his travels, ever come to Bristol? He yearns to meet the fellow in the flesh, shake his hand, take a stroll with him along the quayside and hearken as he tells of his visit to the dark north of the island, or of his adventures in the writing business. But he fears there will be no meeting, not in this life. If he must settle on a likeness for the pair of them, his man and he, he would write that they are like two ships sailing in contrary directions, one west, the other east. Or better, that they are deckhands toiling in the rigging, the one on a ship sailing west, the other on a ship sailing east. Their ships pass close, close enough to hail. But the seas are rough, the weather is stormy: their eyes lashed by the spray, their hands burned by the cordage, they pass each other by, too busy even to wave.

December 7, 2003

The Acceptance Speech

Your Majesties, Your Royal Highnesses, Ladies and Gentlemen; Distinguished Guests, Friends

THE OTHER DAY, suddenly, out of the blue, while we were talking about something completely different, my partner Dorothy burst out as follows: "On the other hand," she said, "on the other hand, how proud your mother would have been! What a pity she isn't still alive! And your father too! How proud they would have been of you!"

"Even prouder than of my son the doctor?" I said. "Even prouder than of my son the professor?"

"Even prouder."

"If my mother were still alive," I said, "she would be ninety-nine and a half. She would probably have senile dementia. She would not know what was going on around her."

■   ■   ■

But of course I missed the point. Dorothy was right. My mother would have been bursting with pride. My son the Nobel Prize winner. And for whom, anyway, do we do the things that lead to Nobel Prizes if not for our mothers?

"Mommy, Mommy, I won a prize!"

"That's wonderful, my dear. Now eat your carrots before they get cold."

Why must our mothers be ninety-nine and long in the grave before we can come running home with the prize that will make up for all the trouble we have been to them?

To Alfred Nobel, 107 years in the grave, and to the Foundation that so faithfully administers his will and that has created this magnificent evening for us, my heartfelt gratitude. To my parents, how sorry I am that you cannot be here.

Thank you.

December 10, 2003

THE WORKS OF J. M. COETZEE

Dusklands

In the Heart of the Country

Waiting for the Barbarians

Life & Times of Michael K

Foe

White Writing

Age of Iron

Doubling the Point: Essays and Interviews

The Master of Petersburg

Giving Offense: Essays on Censorship

Boyhood: Scenes from Provincial Life

The Lives of Animals

Disgrace

Stranger Shores: Essays 1986–1999

Youth: Scenes from Provincial Life II

Elizabeth Costello

J. M. COETZEE was born in 1940 in Cape Town, South Africa, and educated in South Africa and the United States. During an academic career that extended from 1968 to 2002, he held positions in English and comparative literature at a number of universities. His published writings include fiction, literary criticism, memoirs, and translations. He lives in Australia, where he is attached to the University of Adelaide.